REAL LIVES

Alan
Turing

To Lynne, my inspiration

First published 2013 by
A & C Black, an imprint of Bloomsbury Publishing Plc
50 Bedford Square, London WC1B 3DP

www.bloomsbury.com

Copyright © 2013 A & C Black
Text copyright © 2013 Jim Eldridge

ISBN 978-1-4729-0010-4

A CIP catalogue for this book is available from the British Library.

Printed and Bound by CPI Group (UK) Ltd, Croydon CR0 4YY

3 5 7 9 10 8 6 4 2

MIX
Paper from
responsible sources
FSC® C013604

REAL LIVES

Alan Turing

Jim Eldridge

A & C BLACK
AN IMPRINT OF BLOOMSBURY
LONDON NEW DELHI NEW YORK SYDNEY

Contents

1
School

Alan Turing was born on 23 June 1912 in London. At this time his parents lived in India because his father worked for the Indian Civil Service, and soon after Alan was born, his parents returned there. They left their two sons in the care of friends of the family, Colonel and Mrs Ward, who became the boys' foster parents.

This was not unusual for the time. Many British families who worked in India, or other parts of the British Empire, sent their children back to England to be educated, returning occasionally to visit.

Colonel and Mrs Ward lived in St Leonards-on-Sea near Hastings, in Sussex. The upbringing of Alan and his brother was left in the hands of Mrs Ward, but in reality they were brought up by their nanny, who they called Nanny Thompson.

Alan wasn't happy at the Wards: they thought he was a bookish child, rather than an active one, and they disapproved of this. Mrs Ward complained to Alan's mother about this side of him, and Mrs Turing wrote to Alan from India telling him off for being 'too much of a bookworm.'

When Alan was ten, he was sent to Hazelhurst, a small prep school for boys. It was while Alan was there that Julius Turing decided to take early retirement from the Indian Civil Service, and Mr and Mrs Turing moved to the town of Dinard in Brittany in northern France. The plan was for Alan and John to live with their parents in Brittany during school holidays, and return to England during term time to go to school, where they would be boarders (living at the school).

In 1926, Alan sat the entrance exam for a place at Sherborne School. Admission to this prestigious public school was highly competitive. Alan passed the exam and won a place.

In September 1926, Alan, then aged 14, caught the boat from Brittany to Southampton in England, travelling on his own. When he arrived in Southampton there was a General Strike in Britain, which meant there were no trains, no buses, no public transport of any kind. So Alan collected his bicycle from the boat, bought a map, and then cycled the sixty miles from Southampton to Sherborne. On the way he had problems with his bicycle and had to stop to carry out repairs to it, which meant he had to stay overnight at a hotel. Despite this, he cycled in through the gates of Sherborne School in time for the start of school. Being a methodical boy, he posted the receipts for his expenses on his journey to his father in France, asking him to send him the money.

Even at this young age, Alan Turing was a determined person, set on overcoming all obstacles to achieve his aims.

Alan's time at Sherborne was not particularly happy. As at most British public schools at this time, the academic emphasis was on the Classics (Latin and Greek), and on the arts, particularly literature. Sports were also an important feature of school life. Subjects such as sciences and mathematics were looked down on as 'inferior pursuits'. Alan did not enjoy English and Latin: he was bottom of his class in English, and second from bottom in Latin. His handwriting was messy and often illegible. He could not stop his pen from leaking ink and making ink blots on his work. Fellow pupils remembered him as a messy and untidy boy, sometimes stammering when he spoke.

One report from his teacher was very blunt in its disapproval of him, stating, 'His writing is the worst I have ever seen. His work is slipshod, dirty and inconsistent.'

It was hardly an inspiring start for someone who would later be considered to be one of the twentieth century's greatest geniuses.

When it came to sports, Alan did not enjoy team games, although he did enjoy solo long-distance running. It was while he was at Sherborne that Alan's talent as a runner came out, and he won races both at Sherborne and in athletics competitions held against other schools.

Even in mathematics, for which he had shown a great aptitude, Alan had trouble at Sherborne. For one thing, he struggled with long division; but his biggest problem was that he solved mathematical problems without doing any of the early stages that were required: he went straight to the end and reached the correct conclusion without showing how he had arrived at that conclusion. His teachers complained that his work at maths was 'not methodical'. This was seen as very bad: the approved method of working out a maths problem was to build up a proof step by step. Because of this, his work was marked down, and he did badly in maths tests at school.

As far as we know, Alan responded to this with a mixture of annoyance and frustration. He did the work and understood it as well as anyone. When it came to solving mathematical problems, he did not understand why his teachers could not see that he did not need to work out the answer by a long and tedious method, when the correct answer simply leapt out at him. Already, Alan's different way of thinking, a kind of 'lateral' way of working out problems, was showing itself.

Some teachers at the school did see Alan's potential, particularly the chemistry teacher. Chemistry was one of Alan's favourite subjects, and he spent many hours conducting chemistry experiments. In one of these, when he was just 14, he worked out a new method for extracting iodine from seaweed.

It was at Sherborne that Alan finally found a friend he felt comfortable with. Up until the time he met Christopher Morcom, Alan had been a lonely, solitary child, considered anti-social and, because of that, odd. Christopher was a year older than Alan but they were on the same wavelength: both were excited by the mysteries of chemistry and other sciences, as well as enjoying the more complex forms of maths. Alan and Christopher spent a lot of their time discussing Einstein's theories, and working out their own answers to problems that the scientific community were grappling with.

In December 1929, Christopher sat the entrance exam to go to Cambridge University. Alan was keen to go to Cambridge at the same time as Christopher, and also sat the entrance exam, although he was just 17 years old. Christopher passed, his scores being high enough to earn a scholarship. Alan failed, which meant he would have to remain for a further year at Sherborne.

2

Cambridge University

On 6 February 1930, Christopher Morcom became dangerously ill and was rushed to hospital. He was suffering from a recurrence of bovine tuberculosis, the result of drinking contaminated cow's milk many years earlier. On 13 February, Christopher died.

Alan was devastated. He had lost his best – possibly his only – friend.

In December 1930, Alan (now aged 18) again took the entrance exam to try and get a scholarship at Trinity College, Cambridge. He failed. Instead, he was offered a scholarship at Kings College, Cambridge.

His failure to get into Trinity College was lucky for Alan. Kings College, Cambridge was perhaps the best educational institution in Britain as far as mathematics was concerned. The tutors included the mathematician and philosopher, Bertrand Russell, and Max M. H. Newman, mathematician and codebreaker, who was also a pioneer in the world of computers, as well as the world-famous economist, John Maynard Keynes.

Although he was delighted to find himself in an environment where mathematics and science were seen as not just important, but crucial to understanding and explaining all of life, Cambridge was really only enjoyable for Alan as a workplace. As before, socially he was a lonely person. Former graduates who were at Cambridge at the same time as Alan remember him as being shy and awkward. Many commented on his stammer, which became more pronounced when he became excited about something. This was quite probably a case of his brain working faster than his tongue, something often found with people who think very quickly. He could not get out the words fast enough to keep up with the speed at which his brain was working.

He did join the Rowing Club for a while, although his preferred option for sports was still long-distance running, and he continued to win most of the events he ran in.

* * *

Cambridge at this time, the early 1930s, was a hotbed of politics, particularly left-wing politics.

During this period, as Hitler and the Nazis rose to power in Germany and Mussolini in Italy, many young people, particularly students, took an anti-capitalist stance, believing that capitalism was at the core of German and Italian fascism. As a result, many supported the rise of communism, especially as seen in the Soviet Union under Joseph Stalin. Alan was persuaded that his left-wing fellow students had the right idea. In 1933 he wrote to his mother: 'I am thinking of going to Russia some time in vacation. I have joined an organisation called the Anti-War Council. Politically it is rather communist. Its programme is principally to organise strikes among munitions and chemical workers when the government intends to go to war.'

In fact, Alan didn't go to Russia. He also let his membership of the Anti-War Council lapse. The reality was that he had little time for politics, or for anything else except for his interest in science and mathematics.

Despite this, and possibly for the same reasons he failed his exams at Sherborne (putting down the correct answers without showing any working), when he sat the first part of his Final exams he did very badly. He was so embarrassed when his results were published that in a letter to his mother he wrote, 'I can hardly look anyone in the face after it. I shall just have to get a First next time to show I'm not really as bad as those results suggest.'

3

The Thinking Machine

Alan did very well when he re-sat the exam, and he got his First. His work caught the attention of some of the leading mathematicians at Cambridge. John Maynard Keynes, the internationally renowned economist, was impressed by Alan's work, and his unorthodox style. This could be because Keynes had been viewed as a maverick in his younger days, coming up with economic theories that were radical at the time, but which later became part of mainstream economic thought. Also like Alan, Keynes had been marked down and told off for his work at school, which some teachers thought 'careless and lacking in determination'. It is quite likely that Keynes viewed Alan and his maverick attitude to maths research sympathetically.

Keynes gave his backing for Alan to be elected as a Fellow of the College. This was a graduate honour which included a regular income without teaching or lab assistant duties. All Alan had to do was choose a topic for study.

The topic that Alan chose was based on a lecture by Max M. H. Newman, setting out a challenge by the German mathematician David Hilbert. This was the Decision Problem: For any properly constructed mathematical assertion, is there a step-by-step method (an algorithm) that can determine whether the assertion is provable? Hilbert called this 'the principal problem of mathematical logic'.

Alan's aim was to design a machine which would examine every mathematical problem, and attempt to find an answer to that problem by a process of getting every small step on the way to that final solution correct (or 'proved').

His choice of this as a subject is remarkable when one remembers that his maths work had been marked down at both Sherborne, and at Cambridge, because he had *not* detailed the step-by-step methods by which he reached the answers to mathematical problems. Was his search for an answer to Hilbert's Decision Problem a way of analysing and explaining his own methods of deductive thought to himself?

Machines That 'Think'

Alan Turing wasn't the first person to try and create a machine that worked out mathematical problems. The abacus (an early kind of calculator, using beads) was first invented about 4000BC. The first known attempt at building a mechanical machine to solve maths problems is the Antikythera Device, which dates from the first century BC, and which some people believed was designed and built by the famous Ancient Greek scientist, engineer and mathematician, Archimedes.

Across the developed world, Europe, the Middle East and Asia, mathematicians and scientists were intent on creating such a 'calculating' machine. They came in all sizes. One of the smallest appeared in 1622, when William Oughtred invented the slide rule for calculating logarithms.

The first person to design a mechanical calculating machine on a large scale was Charles Babbage, who began designing a mechanical computer in the 1820s. He worked closely on many of his calculations with Ada Byron (the daughter of the poet Lord Byron), a self-taught mathematician. Most of the machines they designed weren't built at the time, because of the cost, but in the 21st century the Science Museum in London built successful working models based on their designs. Interestingly, Babbage is often considered to be 'the father of the modern computer', while Ada Byron (also known as the Countess of Lovelace) was all but written out of the male-dominated history of mathematics. In 1979, Ada Byron was finally acknowledged as the first computer programmer by the United States Department of Defence, who named a key programming language after her: Ada.

Like Babbage and Ada Byron before him, Alan designed his machine in theory, rather than actually building it. During the course of the next year he produced a series of mathematical computations showing the step-by-step stages in dealing with any mathematical problem. When he had finished, he had put down (on paper, at least) the structure and sequences by which a machine could solve the first part of a mathematical problem presented to it, then the next stage, and build on those until the final solution was arrived at – all following a strict sequence of mathematical logic.

Alan wanted more than that. He wanted his 'thinking machine' to be able to find the correct answers to non-mathematical puzzles, using mathematical calculations. For example, in the paradox 'I am lying', is the person who says that actually lying, which means they are telling the truth – or are they telling the truth, which means they are lying?

Alan believed that all these puzzles and paradoxes, as well as mathematical and scientific problems, could be solved by a machine.

At this stage Alan had achieved the first part of his aim. He had designed a machine that worked on a step-by-step method (an algorithm) and could determine whether an assertion was provable. At the age of 23, he had solved David Hilbert's Decision Problem, and developed the step-by-step mechanical basis for the modern computer's calculations.

4

Alan in America

Just as Alan was preparing to publish his paper with his solution to the Decision Problem, from America came news that an American mathematician and logician had also solved the Decision Problem, although using a different method, and had just published his results. He was Dr Alonzo Church, aged 32, a lecturer at Princeton University.

Alan's tutor at Cambridge, Max Newman, got in touch with Church and told him about Alan's work. He suggested that Alan should finish his work on the Decision Problem at Princeton under Church's supervision. Church agreed, and in September 1936, Alan set sail for America, where he joined Church at Princeton University in New Jersey.

Church was very impressed by Alan's work, particularly because he had come to his answer by a very different route from Church's. The result was that Church gave Alan equal credit for solving the problem, and the solution became known as the Church–Turing Thesis.

As had been his situation in Britain, Alan did not get very socially involved in America. His two main colleagues at Princeton were Church and John von Neumann, both mathematical geniuses, and both older than him.

One problem for Alan's social life was that he was gay. Until 1967, it was a criminal offence in Britain for men to have gay relationships. (Gay relationships between women were not illegal.) The playwright Oscar Wilde was sentenced to two years' hard labour in prison in 1897 after being convicted of 'gross indecency' – homosexual acts with another man.

Despite gay relations between men being a crime, there was a certain toleration of homosexuality in some sections of society, a kind of 'don't ask, don't tell' hypocrisy where people pretended not to know. As a result, many openly gay men, such as the playwright Noël Coward and the writer Somerset Maugham, were accepted into the highest levels of society and were never prosecuted. However, many others were prosecuted and sent to prison. To a great extent, it depended on the level of tolerance of different areas of the Establishment, particularly the police force.

In England, Alan made no secret of being gay, especially at Cambridge, where a large number of the tutorial staff were openly gay or bisexual, including John Maynard Keynes. However, Alan was unsure of his position as a gay man in American society. So he avoided creating an active social life for himself, and immersed himself in his work.

It was at Princeton that he began to turn his Thinking Machine into reality, building electro-mechanical components, using a series of multiplications using binary numbers (0 and 1). Alan's theories of mathematical logic were taking their first steps into becoming a real machine.

Von Neumann was particularly impressed by Alan's work and his intellect, and offered him a job as his assistant. But Alan wasn't keen on life in America, and in 1938 he returned to Cambridge and continued his work there. Little did he know that the Second World War and possibly his greatest and most important work were not far away.

5

World War II and the Enigma Code

The First World War ended in 1918 with a defeat for Germany and its allies. The peace was formalised in 1919 with the Treaty of Versailles. There were many in the German military, and some German politicians, who felt that the terms that Germany was forced to accept were not only humiliating, but prevented the country from becoming prosperous again.

Under the terms of the Versailles Treaty, Germany had to formally accept responsibility for the war. It also lost substantial territories: not only its colonial territories overseas (such as those in Africa) but also some of its territories on its own borders (such as those bordering Poland and Austria). Germany also had to pay £6.6 billion (equal to £282 billion in current terms) in compensation to the victorious countries. There were some among the Allies (including Alan's tutor at Cambridge, the economist John Maynard Keynes) who felt that this compensation was too much, and would lead to great hardship and resentment among the Germans, and could lead to Germany going to war again. But the French Government, in particular, insisted on the compensation being paid.

Those in the German military who were determined to make Germany powerful again realised that if they were to take their chances on another war of conquest, they needed their military to be far superior to any possible enemy, and also that they needed improved intelligence and secret communications to prevent the enemy from finding out their plans and operations.

In 1923 Arthur Scherbius, a German inventor and engineer, invented a machine which could be used for high-security communications. He called this machine, and the code it used, Enigma – 'mystery'.

In a simple code or cipher, a letter can be represented by another letter, or a number. For example, in a code where every letter is moved along one space, A becomes B, B becomes C, C becomes D, and so on, and thus the word BAD in code becomes CBE. The problem with simple codes is that they can be broken, and relatively quickly.

The Enigma machine was an electro-mechanical machine, which used rotors to send and receive coded messages. It contained three rotors with 26 electrical contacts on each side (one for every letter of the alphabet). When a key on the keyboard was pressed, an electrical current was sent through the set of rotors. In this way encrypted messages were created and sent by wireless.

In order to decode the messages sent through Enigma, the person receiving the coded message had to know how to set the rotor wheels of the receiving machine so that they matched the position of the sending machine. The positions of the rotors were sent out using a separate code key, and these code keys were listed in a code book kept by all Enigma operators.

Because these codes changed frequently, and because the machine used a mechanical encryption system that had trillions of possible solutions, a message sent from an Enigma machine could really only be deciphered by someone who had not only another Enigma machine but also the current code.

To give you an idea of how hard the Enigma code was to break: three rotors, each with 26 possible correct answers, means that for each encrypted letter there are 26 x 26 x 26 = 17,576 possible solutions. So the possibility of working out the right letter of the code was tiny.

In addition, the Enigma machine had another safeguard: the rotors could be taken out and their sequence altered. When the original 17,576 solutions are multiplied by six (the number of possible wheel orders), that gives 105,456 ways the originating scrambler code could be set up.

By the 1930s, countries who had been enemies of Germany in the First World War had learned about the existence of Germany's Enigma machine and its code, and their intelligence agencies set to work to try and discover how to break the code. They were worried about the rise of Adolf Hitler and his Nazi party. If Hitler came to power and launched another war, then the Enigma code would give Germany a major advantage in secret communications.

In 1932, French agents managed to get hold of an instruction manual for the Enigma machine. They passed it on to the Polish secret service. France and Poland, as countries who shared borders with Germany, saw themselves as most at risk in the event of another war breaking out. The Poles put mathematicians to work on trying to discover from this instruction book how the Enigma machine was wired, and how the rotors worked, and to try and break the code from messages they intercepted.

By the mid-1930s, using the instruction book and mathematical theory, the Polish mathematicians had cracked the Enigma code. Once the Germans became aware of this, in 1938, they developed an even more complicated version of the Enigma machine. The Polish mathematicians found it impossible to break this one at first. But then they came up with a possible answer: using the original Enigma instruction book, they built a machine made up of Enigma rotor assemblies connected together. They called this machine a Bombe.

Like the Enigma machine, the Bombe was an electro-mechanical device. Its task was to identify possible initial positions of the Enigma rotor cores, and the specified series of letters in the correct order, as produced by a set of rotor wheels. In other words, it was intended to be a mirror of the Enigma machine, which would translate the coded gibberish the Enigma machine produced back into the original words.

Using the Bombe, the Poles were able to continue decoding intercepted Enigma messages.

However, once the Germans became aware their messages were being intercepted, they simply added more rotors to their own Enigma machines, going from the original three-rotor version to a four-rotor version, and then a five-rotor version. The more rotors being used to generate the coded message, the greater were the odds against the code being cracked. The Enigma code had become virtually unbreakable.

6

Bletchley Park

So far, the battle between the Germans and the Poles to solve the Enigma code might seem to be just a clash of mathematicians battling for supremacy, trying to outdo one another in an intellectual game – a kind of super-chess. But, once war was declared in September 1939 between Germany and her enemies, especially Britain, it became a battle where millions of lives were at stake.

The entire German military machine depended on Enigma for secret communications, details of troop movements and plans of attack, but the aspect of Enigma that would affect Britain most was related to the German Navy communications.

Every ship in the German Navy had an Enigma machine on board to receive coded intelligence and instructions. This included the small fleets of submarines, called U-boats, that patrolled the Atlantic.

Their aim was to stop merchant shipping between America and Britain. Britain is an island nation and at the start of the war it wasn't able to produce enough food, fuel, weaponry or ammunition for its needs. So, although at the start of the war America was neutral, most of Britain's much-needed supplies came from America. The German plan was to sink these cargo ships to prevent them from reaching Britain. Without these vital supplies, Germany felt confident that Britain would be forced to surrender.

This fear was also shared by the British Prime Minister, Winston Churchill. If Britain could not stop the attacks on the supply convoys by the German U-boat fleets (known as 'wolf packs'), then the country would run out of vital supplies and the war would be lost.

The convoys of cargo ships bringing these supplies across the Atlantic were protected by Royal Navy destroyers, but these were prone to attack from the deep by the wolf packs, who attacked swiftly with their torpedoes, sinking the ships and then vanishing.

The U-boats received details of their targets through the Enigma machine on board, and kept in touch with each other the same way. If the wireless transmissions between the U-boats and their HQ could be unscrambled and deciphered, then the Allies would know what their positions were, which was their next intended target, and when an attack was planned for. They could then take counter-measures to protect the convoy, with warships and planes bombing the U-boat positions. Without that knowledge, every convoy was a row of sitting ducks on thousands of miles of ocean, ripe for a surprise attack.

Cracking the German Naval Enigma code that organised the deadly U-boat wolf packs was absolutely vital if Britain was to survive.

On 4 September 1939, the day after war had been declared between Britain and Germany, Alan Turing reported for duty at Bletchley Park in Bedfordshire. He was 27 years old.

Bletchley Park was a large mansion house set in extensive grounds. Much of the code-breaking work would be carried out in the long single-storey wooden huts that had been set up in the grounds around the main house. Alan was put in charge of Hut 8, where the aim was to crack the German Navy's Enigma coded messages.

Although Alan's intellect had developed since Sherborne and Cambridge, his social skills hadn't. By all accounts he was a solitary person outside work, and cared little for his appearance. There are reports of him keeping his trousers up with string tied round the waist, rather than a belt or braces. A colleague at Bletchley described Alan as 'a tallish dark-haired powerfully built man with sunken cheeks and deep-set blue eyes. He wore unpressed clothes and picked at the flesh around his fingernails until they bled. He stammered and would often fall into long silences. He rarely made eye contact with anyone.'

In the 21st century, someone in such an important position exhibiting these unusual traits of behaviour would probably be examined by psychologists and counsellors to find out why he acted like that, and if he was odd enough to present a danger to the establishment. In recent years, people have tried to understand Alan's rather anti-social manner, suggesting a variety of reasons for how he behaved. Was it because of his separation from his parents at a very early age? The fact that he was gay, and therefore emotionally isolated, because he had to control his feelings so as not to fall foul of the law? Or simply the fact that he felt different because he was cleverer than most people he came into contact with?

It's fascinating to speculate on this now. But in 1939 there was a war on, and nobody had time to worry about what people like Alan were thinking. Britain was in a desperate situation, and it needed everyone to help if the country was going to survive.

The people sent to work at Bletchley came from a variety of interests. There were code-breakers, including mathematicians like Alan, and those with a proven ability to solve puzzles, including chess masters, people who solved cryptic crosswords quickly, and those with similar skills. There were also linguists (for translating intercepted messages in German and other languages), as well as large numbers of people who would intercept and transcribe the wireless transmissions and pass them on to the code-breakers.

One of the first things Alan and the other code-breakers did was to look at the work of the Polish code-breakers, and their code-breaking Bombe machines. They quickly realised that, although these machines had worked well at breaking the early versions of the Enigma code, the additional codes the German had built into their machines meant that any

Bombe built to try and crack it would have to be on a much larger scale than any of the previous Bombes. And, even if they managed to build a big enough Bombe machine, all the Germans had to do was add another rotor or more to their Enigma machine, and the codes would become virtually unbreakable once again, especially considering how fast they had to be deciphered to stop the U-boat attacks in the Atlantic.

When the scale of the problem became apparent, especially when set against its urgency as more and more supply ships were lost, some people in British Intelligence thought the best way to solve the problem was simply to get hold of an Enigma machine. One of these was a Naval Intelligence Officer, Lieutenant Commander Ian Fleming (later to create James Bond), who came up with a plan called Operation Ruthless to try and capture an Enigma machine.

At this time, Fleming was personal assistant to the Director of Naval Intelligence, Rear Admiral John Godfrey. As part of his duties, Fleming visited Bletchley Park twice a month to liaise with Alan Turing and the other code-breakers, and when he outlined his plans for getting hold of an Enigma machine, Alan gave Fleming his enthusiastic support.

This is Fleming's own wording for his plan, which he called 'Operation Ruthless', and which he sent to Rear Admiral Godfrey in September 1940:

I suggest we obtain the loot [an Enigma machine] by the following means:

1. Obtain from Air Ministry an air-worthy German bomber.
2. Pick a tough crew of five, including a pilot, wireless telegraph operator and word-perfect German speaker. Dress them in German Air Force uniform. Add blood and bandages to suit.
3. Crash plane in the Channel after making SOS to [German] rescue service.
4. Once aboard rescue boat, shoot German crew, dump them overboard, bring rescue boat with loot back to English port.

F. 12.9-40. (Fleming. 12 September 1940.)

Fleming had volunteered to be one of the crew of the captured German airplane on this mission, but because of his connection with Bletchley Park it was felt that it was too great a risk if he was captured by the Nazis and interrogated.

A captured German Heinkel was made ready for the mission, and a crew of German-speaking British servicemen were assigned. The plan was to be put into operation at the start of October because it was known that the codes for Enigma were changed at the beginning of every month.

At the start of October, Fleming and his volunteers, along with the Heinkel aircraft, assembled at Dover, waiting for the next German bombing raid, which they would use as cover to launch their own German bomber over the English Channel. However, at the last moment the mission was cancelled.

Alan Turing was so furious at the cancellation that he stormed into the office of his immediate superior at Bletchley Park, Frank Birch, to complain. Birch wrote in a report on 20 October 1940:

Turing and Twinn [Peter Twinn, another mathematician on the team] came to me like undertakers

cheated of a nice corpse two days ago, all in a stew
about the cancellation of Operation Ruthless.

Fleming based his fictional creation of James Bond on himself and his own career in Naval Intelligence. It is interesting to speculate whether the character of Q in the James Bond novels was based on the scientific boffins like Alan at Bletchley Park.

7

Breaking the Code

With the cancellation of Operation Ruthless, there was little chance of Britain getting hold of a real Enigma machine. Time was running out for Britain as the deadly U-boat attacks on the convoys sank more ships and destroyed many more essential supplies.

Many of the scientists at Bletchley Park felt that the Enigma code simply couldn't be cracked. Because it was so complex and with so many permutations, it was thought to be literally unbreakable. Possibly the only two who considered it could be broken were Alan and Frank Birch, the head of Bletchley's Naval Intelligence division. They both believed that the only way to crack the German Naval Enigma code was to design and build a new version of the Bombe. And to do that, they would need to design and build a *thinking* mathematical machine, essentially a continuation of Alan's previous work.

Alan designed a new and advanced version of the Bombe, taking on board important suggestions made by another of his fellow code-breakers at Bletchley Park, Gordon Welchman, who was in charge of Hut 6, responsible for cracking the codes used by the German Army and Air Force. The actual machine was built by an engineer called Harold Keen, working closely with Alan and Gordon.

The way that Bletchley Park worked was as follows: clerks listened in to the wireless traffic between the German commanders and their outposts (including the U-boats) and transcribed the messages, which were in code, and in German.

These messages were passed to the code-breakers, who ran the coded messages through the Bombe machines to try and make the message intelligible, rather than a mass of gibberish.

The problem with cracking the Enigma code was that, although Bletchley intercepted thousands of coded messages every day, the sending machine used an encryption system that had *trillions* of possible solutions, and the key code was changed constantly. In other words, the sheer volume of messages presented to the code-breakers was too large, not just for the code-breakers themselves, but for the Bombe. This meant that the process of trying to break the code was frustratingly slow, and also *dangerously* slow. The more time passed with the Atlantic convoys being lost, the more likely it was that Britain would be forced into surrender.

To try and speed the process up, Alan and the other code-breakers decided to concentrate their attentions on short repeated phrases in the coded messages. They knew that if every German outpost – whether at sea, or on land, or in the air – was sending the same kind of message regularly, then it would very likely be a standard phrase such as 'Nothing to report', 'Weather for the night', or even 'Heil Hitler'. Alan and his fellow code-breakers called these short formulaic messages 'cribs'.

Alan also decided to work on a process of elimination: that is, it is easier to *disprove* a hypothesis than to confirm one. Disproving some possible answers, and thereby eliminating them from any equation, would help reduce the potential workload required in the code-breaking.

Using these methods when examining the coded messages, Alan spotted a weakness in the German

Naval Enigma. The cribs such as 'Wetter fur die nacht' ('Weather for the night'), could be translated by guesswork and could be exploited to follow logical chains, each of which offered billions of possible Enigma settings. If one of these chains led to a contradiction, the billions of corresponding settings on that chain could be eliminated.

However, the odds against finding an answer were still enormous, and a huge number of workers were needed at Bletchley – listeners, transcribers, typists – to examine every coded message that was intercepted, extract these cribs and run them through the Bombes. It was soon realised that the task of sorting through every message and extracting the cribs was too big for the existing numbers of staff. More workers were needed. The problem was that the skilled workers needed to carry out the work were often already at work in other vital areas important to the war effort, so the requests from the Senior Commanders at Bletchley to the War Office for more staff were constantly turned down.

Frustrated, Alan and Gordon Welchman, along with fellow code-breakers Hugh Alexander (who was also the British chess champion) and Stuart

Milner-Barry, decided to take matters into their own hands. They wrote a personal letter to the Prime Minister, Winston Churchill, appealing for the skilled workers needed:

Dear Prime Minister

Some weeks ago you paid us the honour of a visit, and we believe you regard our work as important. You will have seen that we have been well supplied with the Bombes for the breaking of the German Enigma code. We think, however, that you ought to know that this work is being held up, and in some cases is not being done at all, principally because we cannot get sufficient staff to deal with it. Our reason for writing to you direct is that for months we have done everything that we possibly can through the normal channels, and that we despair of any early improvement without your intervention.

This personal appeal to Churchill had an immediate effect. Churchill is on record as saying that preventing the German U-boats destroying the North Atlantic convoys was the single most important element of the Second World War, adding:

'The only thing that ever really frightened me during the war was the U-boat peril.' He knew it was vital that everything must be done to break the Naval Enigma code, and he issued his own memo to the War Office, attached to this letter. It said:

Action This Day. Make sure they [Bletchley Park] have all they want on extreme priority and report to me that this has been done.

Gradually, with more staff identifying the cribs and running them through the Bombes, the Enigma code began to be broken. However, the cracking of the code led to another problem: If the military took action based on the cracked messages, then it could arouse the suspicions of the Germans that their code had been broken, and they might well change the code structure again.

For example, the code-breakers at Bletchley were able to locate the positions of some German supply ships by breaking the coded messages sent to and from the ships. The RAF sent bombers to that location and attacked and sank those ships. Fortunately for the Allies, the Germans felt so secure that the Enigma code was unbreakable that they blamed the successful attack on their ships on espionage, assuming that secret agents must have passed the information about the location of their ships to the Allies.

However, the Germans would not remain so confident if more ships were sunk. So the Allies had to be careful not to use all the information they got from cracking the German wireless messages, in order not to alert the Germans to their success. They used subtle means: if they had discovered the location of a wolf pack of U-boats in the Atlantic from Enigma, they would then arrange for the RAF to fly over that location, as if on a general reconnaissance mission. The attack on the U-boats would then be put down to the U-boats having been spotted by those planes.

At the same time as Alan and his team were breaking the German navy's Enigma code, another team at Bletchley was working on breaking a code known as Tunny, which was used by the German army in Europe. The work this team, especially the cryptoanalayst Bill Tutte, did in breaking Tunny is held by many to be equal to the work carried out by Alan and his team on cracking Enigma. If Tunny could be decoded, the secret transmissions between

Hitler's commanders across Europe could be read, and the actions of his army prepared for. Once Bill Tutte cracked Tunny early in 1942, a new team was set up to continue the work of decoding the Tunny messages. This team was led by Ralph Tester. He, like most of the new Tunny team, came from Alan's unit at Hut 8, and used the techniques and code-breaking skills they had learnt while working under Alan.

* * *

Alan's time at Bletchley also brought him a new relationship – for the first time, with a woman.

Up until he joined Bletchley, Alan had been in mainly all-male establishments. Hazelhurst and Sherborne were both boys-only schools, and the Maths Department at Cambridge had been very much a male enclave. At Bletchley Park, however, although all the senior boffins were men, a large number of women were employed there: some were WRENS (from the Women's Royal Naval Service), and there were also women, many of them from Oxford and Cambridge, who operated the Bombes, and carried out most of the transcription and translating work.

One of the women on Alan's team in Hut 8 was a mathematician called Joan Clarke. For the first time in his adult life, the shy and lonely Alan found he could talk to a woman in an easy manner, without stammering and stumbling over his words. Whether he began to improve his dress sense and stop keeping his trousers up with string at this time is not known, but one thing is sure: Alan and Joan began a relationship.

The fact that she was a mathematician helped enormously, but their friendship was about more than just numbers and calculations; on their days off the two would often go to the cinema, and also go for long bike rides together. As their friendship deepened, Alan asked Joan to marry him, and she agreed. However, once they were engaged, Alan knew he was being unfair to her in not being honest about his sexual nature, and so he admitted to her that he had 'homosexual tendencies', that he was physically attracted to men rather than to women. Possibly to his surprise, Joan told Alan that she was prepared to accept this side of him, and they agreed to get married once the war was over. In the meantime, there was important work to be done.

8

Alan Returns to America

In December 1941, Japanese fighter planes bombed the US Naval base at Pearl Harbour in Hawaii, bringing America into the war.

Now, with America as a legitimate enemy (previously it had been neutral), the Germans began to launch attacks by their U-boat wolf-packs on American ships, and especially on American ships close to America's east coast.

America had never been under attack by submarines before, and as their losses mounted, they realised they needed the help of experienced people if they were to properly defend against the German U-boats. They needed someone who could help them unscramble the coded messages sent to and from the U-boat fleets that lurked off their coast and attacked their ships in the Atlantic. They needed an expert who could help them break the constantly changing Enigma code.

They needed Alan Turing.

In November 1942, Alan was sent by the British by sea to New York. Fortunately, the ship he was on arrived safely, avoiding attacks by German U-boats on its journey across the Atlantic. Alan was immediately sent to the American capital, Washington DC, where the American code-breaking team was based. Alan briefed them on how he and his fellow scientists at Bletchley Park had cracked the Enigma code, but warned them that, as the main codes were altered all the time, attempts at keeping up with the German code had to be constantly updated. If they were going to keep breaking the ever-changing Enigma code, they needed to build Bombes capable of the work.

The Americans, a far richer nation than Britain, responded immediately. Unlike the conditions at Bletchley Park, where money and resources seemed always stretched and barely adequate, the code-breaking system in America swung into action. A factory in Ohio that had produced cash registers for

NCR (the National Cash Register company) began building Bombes for the US Navy to Alan's designs.

The American Bombes were much faster than the British Bombes at Bletchley. One reason was that the drums used in the American machines to drive the rotors rotated at 1,725rpm, which was 34 times faster than the British Bombes.

In the same way that at Bletchley responsibility for decoding messages sent by the Germans was split into Navy (Hut 8 under Alan) and Army and Air Force (Hut 6 under Gordon Welchman), the Americans split their code-breakers into Navy and Army. The Bombe designed for the US Army, although based on Alan's work, was built by Bell Labs and very different from that used by the US Navy. Instead of using rotating drums to represent the Enigma rotors, the Bell Labs version used telephone-style relays. This meant that changing the order of rotors could be done electronically in about half a minute, simply by pushing a button, whereas changing the drum mechanically took about ten minutes.

As well as working with the American cryptographers on cracking Enigma, Alan took advantage of his time in America to investigate other scientific advances that were going on there. He was excited at the work being done at Bell Labs as they attempted to encrypt actual speech. If that could be done, then it would be possible to send secret voice messages, rather than having to send everything in Morse code, or written codes.

Alan also met Claude Shannon, a pioneer of computer science who was based at the prestigious Massachusetts Institute of Technology (MIT). The pair discussed whether a machine could be built that could imitate the action of the human brain. Alan had always believed it was possible to design and make a thinking machine, one that worked on the same logical processes as human thought. Shannon's ideas went even further: he talked about machines being able to read and understand poetry, and listen to and appreciate music.

His meetings in America with Claude Shannon and the scientists at Bell Labs set Alan in a new direction in creating his Thinking Machine, one that would have a major impact on the future of the world.

It was during his visit to Bell Labs that Alan came out with one of his most memorable remarks. While addressing the executives at Bell about his ambition to create a machine that could think, he said: 'I'm not interested in developing a *powerful* brain. All I'm after is just a *mediocre* brain, something like the President of the American Telephone and Telegraph Company.'

This was the company that owned half of Bell Labs. The executives weren't sure whether this was a joke, or an insult, and Alan didn't clarify.

9

Return to Britain

In March 1943, Alan returned to Britain on a troopship. Again, he was lucky it wasn't a target for German U-boats. Possibly he trusted in the fact that by now his colleagues in Hut 8 at Bletchley Park, thanks to the cracking of the Enigma code, had German U-boat movements in the Atlantic under some sort of control.

In his absence, Hugh Alexander, Alan's code-breaking colleague and one of the co-signatories of the letter to Churchill, had taken over the leadership of Hut 8, continuing the work of code-breaking the German naval Enigma. As Alan soon realised, the code-breaking work of Hut 8 was proceeding well, with the Enigma codes being broken and the German's secret messages being read successfully and regularly. To a great extent, Alan was no longer vital to the work of Hut 8.

The commanders at Bletchley Park offered Alan a new code-breaking challenge instead. The Germans were using another code, this one produced by the German Lorenz machine, which the British called Fish. (Tunny was one of the codes produced by this system.) To break this code, a team had designed and built an electronic machine, which they called Heath Robinson, which used two paper tapes. The first tape had on it coded characters from an intercepted message; the other tape had possible wheel patterns from the Lorenz code machine. The paper tape ran through the machine at a thousand characters a second. The main problems with this machine were that the paper tapes often got out of sync, and that the paper often snapped.

Max Newman, one of Alan's former tutors at Cambridge, had looked at the problems affecting the Heath Robinson machine, and he and an electronics engineer called Tommy Flowers had designed and built their own version of the machine, which used patterns generated electronically rather than paper tape. Because of this it was able to process five thousand characters a second. Newman and Flowers called their machine Colossus. It was one of the very first digital electronic computers. Newman invited Alan to join him and Flowers to develop Colossus and give it even greater ability.

Alan declined. The research he had been exposed to in America, particularly the voice encryption work at Bell Labs, inspired him to want to develop a machine that not only had the power of independent thought and decision-making – his Thinking Machine – but one that would be able to communicate using speech. If this could be done and the coded message could be simply listened to as real human speech, then the long job of translating a physical code, letter by letter, as had previously been the case, would be unnecessary.

* * *

Meanwhile, what of Joan Clarke? When Alan had left for America the previous November, there was an understanding between them that they were engaged, and would be married. But perhaps their time apart had given them both time to think about what such a marriage might mean for them, especially in view of Alan's admission to being gay. When they met again on his return to Bletchley, Alan expressed his doubts that a marriage between them would be successful in view of his homosexuality. Joan took his decision with understanding, and the two promised one another they would still be friends. But from that time on, their friendship would never be as deep and close as it had once been.

By all accounts, the ending of his engagement to Joan had little emotional impact on Alan. Possibly theirs had been the kind of 'romance', however ambiguous in its nature, that was kindled during the intensity of war, but once time passed Joan became just another friend in Alan's eyes, and then an acquaintance. Ever since the death of Christopher Morcom, Alan had not really shown any inclination to get deeply emotionally involved with anyone.

Was Alan lonely at this time? Possibly, but he never expressed any feelings of loneliness in his writings, or to his colleagues. To all intents and purposes, Alan's life was poured into his work. He did not appear to need other people.

10
Delilah

After turning down the opportunity to work with Max Newman and Tommy Flowers on their prototype computer Colossus, Alan left Bletchley Park and moved to another Special Operations unit at Hanslope Park, just ten miles away from Bletchley. Like Bletchley Park, Hanslope Park was another country estate with a large historic mansion house. Since 1941 it had been the base for Special Communications Unit Number 3, which researched ways of sending and receiving coded messages.

Inspired by the work he had seen at Bell Labs in America, Alan was determined to create a secure method of communication that used encrypted human speech. Alan's plan was to create and build a machine that could turn human speech into an encrypted form that sounded like static, using a machine called a Vocoder. This 'static' would be unintelligible to anyone listening to it; but when that sound was played through a translator at the receiving end, it would be turned back into intelligible speech.

This was very different from just turning a message into a sound code, such as Morse, where a short bleep (a dot) or a long bleep (a dash) represented a certain letter in the alphabet. Human voices are made up of a mix of sound waves. This means they are analogue, not digital. So first a system had to be worked out to transform this analogue sound into a digital state.

Although this does not sound such a difficult proposition in this digital age, in 1943 electronic engineering was still in its early stages, and the process of finding a way to encrypt human speech would take many months of experiments.

Alan was given two young assistants to help him with his work: Robin Gandy, a mathematician, seven years younger than Alan, and Donald Bayley, an electrical engineer who had just graduated from University. It was Robin Gandy who came up with the name for their project: Delilah.

Finally, in March 1944, Alan and his small team succeeded. They were able to encrypt a recording of a speech made by Winston Churchill, send it as 'static', and then decode it back into its original form.

However, it would take almost a year before Delilah would be fully operational. First the team had to iron out small technical problems with the sound system, to make the sound at the receiver less crackly. By the time Delilah became fully operational, in the spring of 1945, the Second World War was about to end. But all the work that had gone into creating Delilah had not been wasted; it had set the stage for future generations of machines that could communicate using human speech.

11
The Modern Computer Age Begins

On 7 May 1945, Germany surrendered. The War in Europe was over.

In June 1945, Alan was awarded the OBE (the Order of the British Empire) for his services to code-breaking and code-creation during the War. It was generally accepted that his work in cracking the Germans' Enigma code, in particular, had brought about the defeat of Germany much sooner than otherwise would have been the case.

Because of the clandestine nature of his work, the OBE was awarded to Alan in secret, and neither he nor the others at Bletchley Park or Hanslope Park were allowed to say anything about the work they had carried out during the war. By all accounts, this lack of publicity about being awarded the OBE didn't bother Alan in the slightest. According to people who knew him, he simply put the medal in a drawer and then forgot about it. Public accolades and awards didn't interest him: his ambition lay in breaking new boundaries in his work.

However, the secrecy of the work they carried out at Bletchley Park had been a source of embarrassment for many of the young men who worked there during the war. Because the work that was going on at Bletchley had been kept under wraps, many of the people who lived in the towns and villages around the place had developed their own theories about what was going on. A lot of them decided that, although Bletchley Park was officially some sort of Government establishment, it must be some sort of rest home for privileged young men who didn't want to fight in the war. As a result, many of the locals considered the young men to be cowards, hiding away from the action, and treated them as such when they encountered them in the local villages. Other locals, however, began to suspect that *something* was going on at Bletchley Park, once they realised that most of the young men there were mathematicians, chess masters and puzzle solvers.

When the war ended, Alan had decisions to make about his future. One option was for him to return to Cambridge University and become an academic, occasionally lecturing, but mainly conducting mathematical research.

However, Alan wanted to build on the work he had begun, when breaking the Enigma code, in the research he'd seen into the early computers in America, and also with his recent work on Delilah. Alan wanted to build a real and sophisticated Thinking Machine.

In October 1945, Alan joined the staff at the National Physics Laboratory in London, working with the electronic engineers there to create a new breed of computer, using digital technology, and using as a springboard all the mechanical and electronic advances that had happened during the War.

By February 1946, Alan had created a design for an electronic computer – his Thinking Machine – which he called ACE (Automatic Computing Engine). In creating ACE, Alan had realised that the real problem with building an effective Thinking Machine was the *speed* of operation, and the deciding factor in making a machine that worked fast was in its memory. As he wrote in a talk he gave in 1947:

In my opinion this problem of making a large memory available at reasonably short notice is much more important than that of doing operations such as multiplication at high speed. Speed is necessary if the machine is to work fast enough for the machine to be commercially valuable, but a large storage is necessary if it is to be capable of anything more than trivial operations.

Although Alan's time at the National Physics Laboratory should have been one of excitement and fulfilment, with the NPL electronics engineers putting his designs and theories into practical form, in reality Alan was frustrated there. For one thing, there was a constant lack of funds, which affected the development of his ideas. Immediately after the war, Britain was suffering economically, and the Government opted to spend what little money it could get on rebuilding the bomb-damaged country.

Alan was also upset at the levels of bureaucracy at NPL, which interfered with his work. He was constantly being forced to attend meetings, and produce organisational paperwork that had little to do with his actual research. Although Alan gained a lot by working in small teams, such as the Hut 8 code-breaking team at Bletchley, and the small three-man team who developed the Delilah project, he was not a 'company' person. Bureaucracy and paperwork, especially when he considered it unnecessary and interfering with really important scientific work, annoyed and frustrated him.

So, when, in 1947, he was offered a chance to return to King's College, Cambridge for pure academic research for a year, he took it.

12

A Computer Called Baby

It was while he was at NPL that Alan started competitive long-distance running again. In 1946 he became a member of the Walton Athletic Club, based in Walton, Surrey. Such was his ability at long-distance running, including marathons, that he was considered as a serious candidate for the British athletics team for the 1948 Olympics. Unfortunately, during this period (1946–8) he suffered an injury which meant he would not be fit for the Olympics, and put an end to his competitive running career.

However, 1948 was to mark a major new chapter in his scientific career.

During his year at Cambridge, Alan was invited to join a brand new project at the University of

Manchester, aimed at developing a new kind of computer. The machine was called the Small Scale Experimental Machine or SSEM – though it was called Baby by everyone involved with the project. In May 1948, when his sabbatical year at Cambridge ended, Alan joined the team at Manchester.

At the heart of Baby was the importance of the amount of memory it could store, just as Alan had emphasised in his talk in 1947. The SSEM used a device known as the Williams tube to store computer data. The Williams tube had been invented during the war by Frederick Williams as a means of storing radar images of ships and planes in a cathode ray tube. The images were kept bright and easily visible in the cathode tube by means of electronic pulses passed through the tube. The radar image on an ordinary screen would appear, and then fade. The Williams tube kept those images alive and available in the machine's memory.

The Williams tube was able to store data at 2Kb (2,000 bits), which at that time was a massive amount of storage. (To put this in context, the computer that powered the Apollo space mission in 1969 had a memory of 64Kb. Computer memory has expanded hugely since then: the memory of a modern smartphone is 256Mb.)

The first program for the SSEM was written by a computer engineer called Tom Kilburn, and was run in June 1948. The program was a mathematical one, aiming to find the highest factor of 2^{18} (262,144), using every integer from 1 to 262,144. To do this, the SSEM had to carry out 3.5 million operations. The operating time for this program was 52 minutes, and at the end the machine had calculated the answer as 131,072 (i.e. half of 262,144).

It was not the answer that created the excitement, but the fact that the *machine* had calculated it, and had done so by carrying out 3.5 million calculations in so short a time.

Alan arrived at Manchester University towards the end of Tom Kilburn's successful program using Baby. The question was, what could he contribute to the project? The machine had already been created, with Frederick Williams' memory device at its heart, and programmers such as Tom Kilburn writing complex maths programs for it. But Alan wanted to see if he could develop Baby to replicate the biological functions of the brain. He wanted to create a machine that wasn't just a fast-acting supersonic calculating machine, but a device that could reason, and reach a conclusion about a problem – *any* problem, including artistic or literary issues as well as scientific ones. Alan was aiming to develop something capable of artificial intelligence.

13
AI

In October 1950 Alan published one of his most famous articles, in the magazine *Mind*. It was called 'Computing Machinery and Intelligence' and began: 'I propose to consider the question: Can machines think?'

Alan went on to describe the problems that he felt a machine, properly programmed, could deal with. To back up his proposition, he put forward what became known as the Turing Test. In this theoretical test, a person (A) was stationed at a computer terminal which was linked to two other terminals, and posed questions by means of sending text. One of the other terminals was controlled by a person, who sat at the keyboard and responded to the questions posed. The other terminal was a computer that answered the questions sent to it with no human interference. Replies from both terminals were also in text.

The Turing Test is whether the person who was asking the questions (A) could decide from the answers which of the two responding terminals was operated by a human being, and which by a computer.

According to Alan: 'If, during text-based conversations, a machine is indistinguishable from a human, then it could be said to be thinking, and therefore could be attributed with intelligence.'

The sample questions that Alan used as examples for the Turing Test included the following exchanges between A and the two unseen recipients (along with the answers received by A from them):

Q: Please write me a sonnet on the subject of the Forth Bridge.
A: Count me out on this one. I never could write poetry.
Q: Add 34957 to 70764.
A: (After a pause of about 30 seconds) 105,621.
Q: Do you play chess?
A: Yes.
Q: I have K (King) at my K1, and no other pieces. You have only K (King) at K6 and R (Rook) at R1. What do you play?
A: (After a pause of about 15 seconds) R–R8 Mate.

If these questions and the answers are examined and thought about, it can be seen that any of the answers could have come from a human being *or* a machine, including the one in response to writing a sonnet about the Forth Bridge: 'Count me out on this one. I never could write poetry.'

In this same article, Alan went on to say: 'I believe that in about 50 years time it will be possible to program computers so well that an average interrogator will have no more than a 70% chance of making the right identifications after five minutes of questioning.'

It was with this article that Alan started up a whole debate about Artificial Intelligence, not just among the scientific community, but among religious leaders and theologians as well. This was because most organised religions have as their basis the idea that God created human beings, and their capabilities. If a machine could be created that could think and reason in the same way as a human being, then that took away the idea of reasoning beings as only 'created by a God, a divine being'.

14

Fibonacci Numbers and Order in the Universe

If Alan had upset some of the most religious people with his claim that machine intelligence equal to human intelligence could be created by scientists such as himself, the next phase of his mathematical theories might have confused many. It examined the connection between mathematics and plants, and his research suggested a link between plants and a kind of Mathematical Designer and Creator, although he did not assert this conclusion directly.

His research centred around the patterns on sunflower heads. Alan had noticed that seeds on sunflower heads were arranged in a spiral pattern that followed what was known as the Fibonacci sequence.

In the Fibonacci sequence, each number is the sum of the previous two numbers, starting with 0 and 1. The sequence begins:

0, 1, 1, 2, 3, 5, 8, 13, 21, 34, 55, 89, 144, 233, 377, 610, 987 ... and so on.

Leonardo Fibonacci was a thirteenth-century Italian mathematician. He was not the first to spot the sequence's occurrence in nature, but he was the first to bring it to the attention of the Western world. The first known observation of this sequence of numbers occurring regularly in nature was found in in ancient India, in the Sanskrit language. Versions appear in the Hindu-Arabic number systems.

Leonardo Fibonacci's father was a merchant who travelled around the Arabic world, often taking Leonardo with him. It was on these journeys that Leonardo became aware of the number sequence that occurred so frequently in plants, and in other forms of nature. Leonardo studied mathematics under the leading Arab mathematicians of the time, and in 1202, at the age of 32, he published what he had learnt in a book called *Liber Abaci* (*The Book of Abacus*, also known as *The Book of Calculations*).

The theory that plants, and other aspects of nature, had a mathematical basis to their construction was widely discussed. Leonardo da Vinci studied this phenomenon, and many other mathematicians and scientists from ancient times had made the same observation. Shapes in nature where the spiral form could be defined by the Fibonacci sequence of numbers include the growth of mollusc shells, the shapes of many flowers and fruits (including pineapples and artichokes), the uncurling of fern fronds, the distribution patterns of branches on tree trunks, and the shape of pine cones. In modern times, the Fibonacci sequence has even been detected in the construction of DNA.

Before computers, these discoveries had been the result of physical examination of plants, as scientists counted the facets that made up the spiral shapes. Now Alan was able to apply technology to the problem, using a computer to positively identify the arithmetical Fibonacci sequence in the spiral forms of sunflower heads.

However, when, in 1952, he published his paper linking the spiral forms of the sunflower heads to the Fibonacci sequence, it was still only a theory.

It was not until 2012 – a hundred years after Alan's birth – that his theory was properly investigated and evaluated by the Museum of Science and Industry with the launch of the Turing Sunflowers Project, in which 12,000 people from seven different countries donated sunflower specimens for examination. At the time of writing (March 2013), of the sunflower heads examined and analysed in the Project, 82% had their seeds arranged in a spiral pattern in which the number of rows of seeds followed the Fibonacci sequence.

The implication of Turing's theory, following those of the Hindu-Arab scholars, Fibonacci, Leonardo da Vinci, and sundry others, is that the elements in nature have not emerged haphazardly, but have a mathematical basis. If that is the case, where did this mathematical basis come from? Did these elements in nature that follow the Fibonacci sequence develop these spiral forms under some pressure of evolution? Or were they designed by some mysterious force?

To some people, the idea that Alan Turing – renowned as a purely analytical scientist, a mathematician – should be involved in something that suggests a 'creator' at work appears very inconsistent with his previous research and work. It is often assumed that hard science and spirituality do not have a common ground. Certainly there is no evidence that Alan was interested in any organised or traditional religion. The concept of an all-powerful God does not appear in his work, or his life.

However, there is a lot of evidence of Alan's interest in what could be called spirituality, or non-physical influences in the world.

The first traces of this can be found in Alan's writings and letters following the tragic death of his close friend, Christopher Morcom, in 1930. In a letter to his mother shortly after Christopher died, Alan wrote: 'I feel I shall meet Morcom again somewhere and that there will be work for us to do together.'

In a paper he wrote at this time called 'Nature of Spirit', he said: 'The body, by reason of being a living body, can attract and hold onto a spirit. While the body is alive and awake the two are firmly connected. When the body is asleep I cannot guess what happens, but when the body dies the mechanism of the body holding the spirit is gone and the spirit finds a new body sooner or later, perhaps immediately.'

This may seem like an anti-scientific stance, but in fact it was very much part of the sciences that were emerging at that time, particularly in the areas of quantum physics, where practically anything was considered possible, including the idea of parallel universes existing at the same time, and the concept of a soul or spirit leaving the physical body (called an 'out-of-body experience').

Further evidence of the continuation of Alan's interest in and acceptance of what are sometimes termed 'alternative sciences' or 'the paranormal' come in his explanatory notes to his Turing Test at Manchester in 1950. He wrote: 'Unfortunately the statistical evidence, at least for telepathy, is overwhelming. ... Let us play the imitation game (aka the Turing Test) using as witnesses a man who is a good telepathic receiver, and a digital computer. The interrogator can ask such questions as 'What suit does the card in my right hand belong to?' The man, by telepathy or clairvoyance, gives the right answer 130 times out of 300 cards. The machine can only guess at random, and perhaps gets 104 right.'

From all of this, as well as his interest in the Fibonacci number sequence in nature, it does suggest that Alan believed there was more to life and the universe than what we could *physically* see or experience. In this he was no different to those earlier scientists who insisted on the existence of electricity in the atmosphere, or magnetism – both scientific facts but which could not be seen by the general observer. In our own time, it is the same with the discovery of black holes, which were considered theoretical at first but subsequently proved to exist. Many now-proven scientific facts were at first dismissed as supernatural.

It is my view that with all of this, Alan was trying to find scientific causes for *everything*. His research and investigation over many years into the act of reasoning, using machines to explain and recreate the process, were just a part of his trying to explain the bigger question: is there a form of order and structure in the universe?

15

Arrested and Tried

Alan's 1952 publication showing the connection between Fibonacci numbers and sunflower heads could have led him to even greater discoveries in his overall quest for the bigger questions about the structure of the Universe. But, in 1952, something happened that changed the course of his life dramatically, and, some believe, led to his early death.

As we have seen, from early in his life, since his teens, Alan had realised that he was gay. He never deliberately kept his homosexuality a secret. As we have seen, at Bletchley Park he met and became engaged to Joan Clarke, but he did warn her that he had 'homosexual tendencies'. Once he had got to know his co-workers, he often revealed the fact that he was gay to them. Many of his friends and co-workers simply accepted it and got on with working with him. Others reacted badly. This was the case when he told Donald Bayley, his teamworker on the Delilah Project, that he was gay. Whether because being gay was illegal or Bayley's own prejudice, his initial reaction was one of disgust, and for a time it put a strain on their relationship. Eventually Bayley came to accept Alan's sexuality as just one part of him, and they became good friends.

In December 1951, Alan met a young man called Arnold Murray in Manchester, and they began a relationship. Murray came from a tough working-class background. At the time that Alan met him, Murray was broke, out of work, shabbily dressed, and very thin from a lack of proper food. He was a very different character from men Alan had known previously, most of whom came from his own kind of background: middle class family, public school and university.

Alan and Murray spent a lot of time together at Alan's small semi-detached house in Manchester, and Alan started giving Murray money to help him out.

In January 1952, Alan's house was burgled, and he was shocked to discover that an acquaintance of Murray's, a man called Harry, had carried out the burglary. Alan reported the burglary to the police, and Harry was arrested. He confessed to the burglary, but told the police about Alan's relationship with Murray, possibly in the hope that giving evidence about their criminal relationship might get him a lighter sentence.

Because male homosexuality was illegal, most men suspected or accused of being gay would deny it. Often this denial was accepted, even if the truth was known, provided it could not be proved. Frequently, the only way a case was proved was when the men involved admitted to taking part in homosexual acts, and this rarely happened, as the men would not want to go to prison. In the 1895 case of Oscar Wilde, for example, most of Society at that time knew he was gay, but they were happy to turn a blind eye to it. He was not arrested until the father of one of his lovers gathered evidence against him and sent it to Scotland Yard.

However, in the early 1950s, there was an increasing clampdown on homosexual acts. Homosexuality was now seen as a danger to society. Undercover police officers acting as *agents provocateurs* would pretend to be gay and arrest the men they entrapped, and the police pursued cases much more actively.

In the case of Alan's relationship with Murray, the police put Harry's accusations about their sexual relationship to both men. If Alan and Murray had lied and denied it, that might have been the end of the matter. However, when the police asked Alan about his relationship with Murray, Alan admitted that it was sexual. Both men were charged with gross indecency.

At Alan's trial, where he pleaded guilty, his barrister asked that Alan be spared a prison sentence, telling the judge: 'The public would lose the benefit of the research work he is doing [if he were sent to prison]. I ask you to think that the public interest would not be well served if this man is taken away from the important work he is doing.' The barrister added: 'There is a treatment which could be given to him.'

This 'treatment' was a course of 'chemical castration'. This was based on the theory that regular injections of oestrogen (the female sex hormone) would reduce Turing's sex drive and make him lose interest in sex with men.

The judge agreed that Alan could be put on probation instead of going to prison, provided he agreed to submit to this chemical castration. Alan agreed to this course of action. However, because he was found guilty and convicted of a homosexual offence, his official security clearance was cancelled. (Because being gay was a crime, homosexuals were considered vulnerable to blackmail by enemy agents.) For Alan, it meant that he could no longer be consulted on any top secret code-cracking issues.

There are conflicting views from people who knew Alan at this time about how he was affected by what happened. There were those who feel that it had little emotional impact on him at all, that he accepted the course of injections and was almost dismissive of it. Certainly, as there had been no restrictions on his travelling out of the country during his period of probation, Alan took trips abroad to France and Greece through the summer of 1953, and by all accounts enjoyed these trips.

However, others felt that the ban on him working for the Government on any sort of top secret research, whether code-breaking or advanced development in the area of computers, hit Alan hard. Such research and investigation had been his life, his enjoyment, and to find that world barred to him would have been particularly painful.

There was another, physical issue, that upset him. As a result of the course of injections of oestrogen, Alan developed larger breasts. He also put on weight. For someone who had always been a keen, fit and lean athlete, this was depressing.

16
Death

By the end of 1953, Alan had completed his term of probation, and his course of chemical treatments. Although he could no longer be employed on top secret Government work, the Science Department at Manchester University extended his contract for at least another five years.

He was also still intrigued by the potential for artificial intelligence and keen to do more work on that. He also wanted to extend the work he'd done on his Sunflowers Project, and extend it into the field of molecular biology.

In 1954 he also began writing fiction. His first story was obviously based on his own experiences and his relationship with Murray. The hero is Alec, a scholarly man who falls into a relationship with a young man called Ron: 'Ron had been out of work for two months and he'd got no cash.'

This story was never finished. On 8 June 1954, Alan's housekeeper, Mrs Clayton, found him dead in his bed. On the bedside table was an apple which had several bites taken out of it. The apple was found to contain traces of cyanide.

The inquest into Alan's death was held just two days later, on 10 June. The coroner's verdict was that Alan Turing had committed suicide by means of an apple poisoned with cyanide.

What led the coroner to reach this verdict? Certainly, the turmoil of events in his recent life could have pointed to that conclusion: his arrest and trial for gross indecency, the chemical castration he endured, his time on probation, being barred from the kind of Government research work he loved: all of these could have led to him being depressed.

Many people close to Alan disagreed with this verdict. His mother insisted that he would never have taken his own life. There was evidence from those who saw him in the last few days of his life that he showed no signs of depression, or wanting to kill himself. Alan's neighbour, Mrs Webb, said, 'Alan invited me and my husband to dinner on June 1st, and we spent a delightful evening with him. I saw him several times during the next two days and he was very jolly. Alan was full of plans for coming to visit us on his way home from the University in the afternoons.'

Alan's housekeeper, who saw him regularly at this time, also said that she couldn't believe that Alan had deliberately killed himself. The view of many of those close to him was that Alan had got his life under control. Since finishing his course of oestrogen injections, he had lost weight and got himself fit again. He was enjoying writing. He was engaged on work that he liked at Manchester University. Why would he want to kill himself?

But if Alan did not kill himself, how had he died? And why had the apple on his bedside table been contaminated with cyanide?

Alan's mother, Ethel Turing, was sure that his death had been a tragic accident. Alan had always liked carrying out chemistry experiments, and he had a stock of chemicals at his house, including cyanide. It was also known that Alan liked to eat an apple before going to bed at night. In his mother's view, Alan had got some cyanide on his fingers while carrying out an experiment, and the cyanide had got onto the apple. She was supported in this view by a psychoanalyst called Dr Greenbaum, who Alan had contacted to discuss his homosexuality. A letter from Dr Greenbaum to Ethel Turing said: 'There is not the slightest doubt to me that Alan died by an accident. You describe Alan's fashion of experimenting [with chemicals] so vividly that I can see him pottering about. He was like a child while experimenting, always testing things with his fingers.'

Another theory has been put forward. In the early 1950s, after the defection of two British spies to Soviet Russia, it was suspected that there was a spy ring made up of former Cambridge students, centred on those who had been at Trinity and King's Colleges during the 1930s. Alan went to King's, and joined the communist-sympathising Anti-War Council there. He had knowledge of top secret information at the highest level. Some people have therefore speculated that he was killed by the security forces in case he defected, and his death staged to look like suicide.

So: suicide, accident, or even murder? The debate still rages.

17
Alan's Legacy

One thing is certain: although Alan Turing is considered by many to be 'the father of the modern computer', his enduring fame will always be as The Genius at Bletchley Park Who Broke The Enigma Code.

The work Turing and the Bletchley Park code-breakers did in cracking the Enigma code is thought by experts to have shortened the war in Europe by as many as two to four years.

Captain Jerry Roberts of the Royal Navy went further: 'In 1940 the German U-boats were sinking our food ships and our ships bringing in armaments, left, right and centre, and there was nothing to stop this until Turing managed to break the naval Enigma as used by the U-boats. We then knew where the U-boats were positioned in the Atlantic and our convoys could avoid them. If that hadn't happened, it is entirely possible, even probable, that Britain would have been starved and would have lost the war.'

Many people agree that without Turing's work on breaking the German codes, Nazi Germany might have won the Second World War.

On 10 September 2009, in response to a petition asking the British Government to posthumously apologise to Alan Turing for prosecuting him for being gay, the British Prime Minister Gordon Brown issued the following official statement about Alan's trial and sentence.

It is no exaggeration to say that without Alan Turing's outstanding contribution, the history of World War II could well have been very different. The debt of gratitude he is owed makes it all the more horrifying, therefore, that he was treated so inhumanely. In 1952 he was convicted of 'gross indecency' – in effect, tried for being gay. His sentence – and he was faced with the miserable choice of this or prison – was chemical castration by a series of injections of female hormones. He took his own life two years later.

Thousands of people have come together to demand justice for Alan Turing and recognition of the appalling way he was treated. While Turing was dealt with under the law of the time and we can't put the clock back, his treatment was of course utterly unfair and I am pleased to have the chance to say how deeply sorry I and we all are for what happened to him. Alan, and many thousands of other gay men who were convicted as he was under homophobic laws, were treated terribly. Over the years, millions more lived in fear of conviction.

It is thanks to men and women who were totally committed to fighting Fascism, people like Alan Turing, that the horrors of the Holocaust and of total war are part of Europe's history and not Europe's present.

So, on behalf of the British Government, and all those who live freely thanks to Alan's work, I am proud to say: We're sorry, you deserved so much better.

It is fascinating to conjecture what Alan Turing might have achieved, what new breakthroughs and developments in computer sciences he might have made, if he had not died at the relatively young age of 41.

He pioneered and developed the Thinking Machine, machines that spoke and understood human speech; he developed Artificial Intelligence; he pushed the boundaries of computer science every step of the way, always searching for the next step. Where next? The hybrid human-organic-computer? A machine that designs and replicates itself?

In fact, both of these proposals are being developed and refined, as are many other developments in technology; and many in the scientific community consider that these advances have been made possible because of the groundbreaking work of Alan Turing.

Such has been Alan Turing's impact on the world of science and mathematics, that his memory and work has been celebrated with many honours in his name, and buildings named after him.

- In the early 1960s, Stanford University in America named the lecture room at the Polya Hall Mathematics building 'Alan Turing Auditorium'.

- Since 1966, the Association for Computing Machinery has given an annual Turing Award for technical or theoretical contributions to the computing community. It is generally acknowledged as the computing community's highest honour.
- In 1994, a stretch of the A6010 road, the Manchester city intermediate ring road, was named Alan Turing Way.
- In 1999, Time magazine named Alan as one of the Most Important People of the 20th Century.
- In June 2001 a statue of Alan Turing was unveiled in Sackville Park in Manchester. The statue shows Alan sitting on a bench made of cast bronze. He is holding an apple. The text on the bench reads: 'Alan Mathison Turing. 1912–1954.' There then follows the motto: 'Founder of Computer Science', but in the form it would appear in if it had been encoded by an Enigma machine: IEKYF RQMSI ADXUO KVKZC GUBJ.
- The University of Texas at Austin has an honours computer science programme named the Turing Scholars.
- Istanbul Bilgi University in Turkey organises an

Annual Conference on the theory of computation called Turing Days.

- One of the two amphitheatres of the Computer Science Department at the University of Lille in France is named in honour of Alan Turing.
- The University of Oregon, USA, has a bust of Alan Turing on the side of their computer science building, the Deschutes Hall.
- The Ecole Polytechnique Federale de Lausanne in Switzerland has a road and a square named after Alan (*Chemin de Alan Turing* and *Place de Alan Turing*).
- The University of Surrey has a statue of Alan Turing on their main piazza.
- At Edinburgh's School of Informatics there is a Turing Room, with a bust of Alan.
- There are Departments of Computer Sciences named after Turing at many universities, including Chile, Puerto Rico, Bogota, Turin, Keele University, Bangor, Ghent, Lille in France, Oregon (USA), Aarhus (Denmark), and, of course, Cambridge, England.

The legacy of Alan Turing lives on.